This book belongs to

_____

ON MY WAY
WITH
SESAME STREET ™

Volume 15

Summer, Fall, Winter, Spring

Featuring the Sesame Street Characters

Children's Television Workshop/Funk & Wagnalls

Authors

Tony Geiss
Michaela Muntean
Rae Paige
Pat Tornborg

Illustrators

Tom Cooke
Tom Leigh

0-8343-0089-3   5 6 7 8 9 0

A Parents' Guide to
SUMMER, FALL, WINTER, SPRING

Learning about the four seasons is one way to help children understand many pre-science subjects. SUMMER, FALL, WINTER, SPRING presents changes that occur in the weather, environment, plants, and animals throughout the year. It also shows how people respond to these seasonal changes in their dress and activity.

''The Runaway Hat'' is a delightful story about one spring day when Ernie's hat is blown away and becomes a nest for some baby birds. Ernie visits the nest from spring to fall and observes the changes that occur.

''The Four Seasons'' is a funny play in verse performed by the Sesame Street Players: Bert personifies winter; Herry, spring; Ernie, summer; and Cookie Monster, fall.

''Grover's Pond'' is a continuing activity that shows what happens to plant and animal life throughout the year.

The ''Spring,'' ''Summer,'' ''Autumn,'' ''Winter'' pictures depict the same back yard scene throughout the four seasons. Point out to your child how the apple tree, the garden, the family's clothing, work, and play change in the pictures. Then point out seasonal changes in your own back yard.

Observing the cyclical nature of the four seasons helps your children to understand the passage of time and to anticipate what happens from one season to the next.

The Editors
SESAME STREET BOOKS

The Runaway Hat

Ernie's favorite hat is the one that Bert gave him.

One spring afternoon Ernie put on his favorite hat and went for a walk in the park. There were tiny new green leaves on the trees. There were red and yellow tulips in the flower beds.

The wind began to blow. At first it was a gentle breeze and soft as a whisper. But then the wind grew stronger, and it blew harder and harder.

Ernie felt a sudden gust and reached up to hold his hat on his head, but he was not as fast as the wind. The wind blew his hat right off his head and lifted it into the air.

"Stop!" Ernie cried as he ran after his hat. "Don't run away, hat!" But his hat did not stop, and the wind did not stop. It blew harder and harder, and it carried Ernie's hat away, higher and higher in the air.

Ernie looked and looked, but he could not find his hat. "It has to be around here somewhere," he said. "Hats do not just disappear!"

It was getting late. Ernie was cold, and tired, and hungry. "Wherever you are, blue hat," Ernie shouted into the wind, "stay there! I will be back to find you tomorrow."

His head felt very lonely without his hat as he walked home sadly to Sesame Street.

Ernie came back the next day to look for his hat. He came back the day after that, and the day after that, too. And every day Ernie looked in a different place.

He looked under park benches and picnic tables and trash cans. He looked over fences and hedges and gates. Ernie looked around and through and in everything he could think of, but he did not find his hat.

"I give up," Ernie said, sighing, and he sat down under a large oak tree. Just then a robin began to sing. Ernie looked up and saw the robin in the tree. He also saw... his hat!

"I'm coming to save you," Ernie called to his hat, and he climbed up the tree as quickly as he could. But when he reached the limb, there was something in Ernie's hat, and it was not a head. "Bert will never believe this!" said Ernie. The robin had built a nest in Ernie's hat, and in the nest were three beautiful blue eggs.

"What a silly nest!" said Ernie. "I can't take my hat back until the mother robin's eggs are hatched."

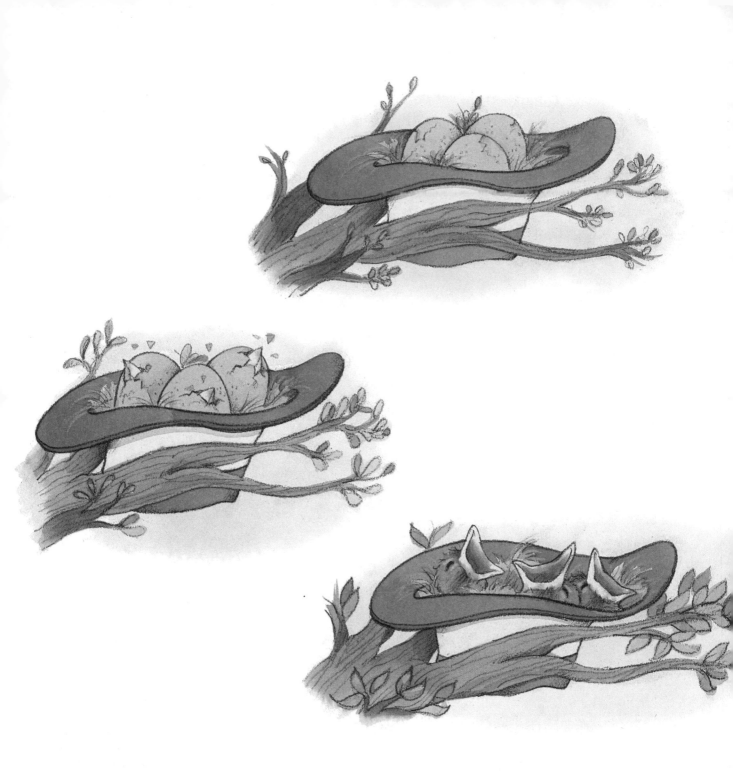

So every day Ernie went to the park to visit his hat. Soon he saw cracks in the eggshells. Then he saw beaks breaking through the cracks. Finally the baby robins came out of the shells.

"Wow!" said Ernie. "I can't take my hat back until the baby birds are bigger."

So Ernie sat in the tree and watched as the mother bird brought her babies wiggly worms to eat. *Cheep, cheep,* the baby birds sang.

Day after day Ernie waited and Ernie watched. The baby birds grew bigger and stronger.

"I can't take my hat back until the babies are big enough and strong enough to fly away," he said.

Summer was almost over, and the days were growing shorter.
The leaves began to turn red and orange and yellow.

Then one day when Ernie went to visit his hat, the oak tree was
quiet. The nest was empty.

Ernie sat in the tree and waited, but the birds did not come.

"The bird family must have gone to a warm place for the
winter," said Ernie sadly.

"Well, at least I can have my hat back now!" he said.

Ernie carried the hat down from the tree. He shook out all the
twigs. And out fell a long, beautiful feather.

"Bert will never believe this!" said Ernie. "The birds left a
present for me." And he put the feather in the band of his hat.

The wind was blowing as Ernie walked home to Sesame Street,
and this time he held on to his hat.

Grover's Pond

"Oh, my goodness! Look at those cute little baby ducks in the pond. They are swimming behind their mother."

Point to the duck that doesn't belong.

Then take Grover to the other side of the pond to see what he will find there.

"Oh, look who lives on this side of the pond! There are frogs and tadpoles. Can you see the tadpoles in the water? Tadpoles look like little fish with long tails, but do you know what they really are? They are baby frogs! They will grow up to look just like this big green frog on the lily pad."

How many tadpoles can you find in the water? Count them.

6

Helping Around the House

closet

mop

bucket

Ernie and Bert clean up their room.

broom

dustpan

Big Bird sweeps the steps.

pillow

bedspread

The Twiddlebugs make the bed.

glass

cup

plate

fork

spoon   knife

Grover sets the table.

It's clean-up time on Sesame Street.
What jobs do you help with around the house?

feather duster

cloth

spray bottle

Snuffie dusts the ceiling.

Betty Lou shines the mirror.

soapsuds

rubber gloves

sponge

dishtowel

Cookie Monster washes the dishes. Frazzle dries them.

clothesline

dryer

washing machine

blanket

vacuum cleaner

The Count vacuums the rug.

Oscar folds his laundry.

A Rainy Day

"Drip, drop, splish, splash.
When I hear that sound I know
The rain is here to help
The plants and flowers grow."

Ernie is going for a walk in the rain.
Point to the things that will help keep him dry.

"Drip, drop, splish, splash.
 When I hear that sound I know
 The rain is here to help
 The muddy puddles grow!

"Wow, look at all those big muddy
 puddles! Grouches aren't the only ones
 who love mud. Worms love mud, too."

How many worms can you find in this picture? Count them.

10

This is the Monster family's back yard. It is a windy spring day.
Can you find the robin and her nest?

Spring

chimney

telephone pole

kite

house

garage

fence

car

window box

picnic table

forsythia

maple tree

shrubs

shovel

seeds

stake

hoe

crocus

lawn

lawn mower

dock

robin

nest

toy sailboat

turtle

ducklings

duck

mud

pond

apple tree

daffodils

violets

fern

pussy willows

It's hot. The little Monsters go swimming to cool off.
What game is Cookie Monster playing?

Summer

lemonade

watermelon

barbecue grill

zinnias

bat

baseball

vegetable garden

underwater mask

water wings

sunglasses

baseball glove

flippers

diver

swimmer

fish

cattails

frog

lily pad

water lily

It's cool and the leaves are starting to fall.
How many apples have fallen on the ground?

geese

Autumn

pumpkin

rake

cider

corn stalks

leaves

football
helmet

football

soccer ball

apples

squirrel

acorn

It's cold and snowy. Everyone bundles up.
Where is Rubber Duckie?

Winter

icicle
toboggan
skis
hat
snow blower
sled
top hat
snowball
broom
snowsuit
parka
boots
snowman
scarf
earmuffs
mittens
puck
snow shovel
ice skates
hockey stick
ice

Grover's Pond

"I, Grover, am here to tell you how everyone is doing at the pond. Look how big the baby ducks have grown! Do you know what ducks say? They say, *quack, quack!*"

"Oh, look! The baby ducks think I am a duck, too."

How many ducks are following Grover? Count them. Grover and the baby ducks left their footprints in the mud around the pond. Follow the path they made to the other side of the pond.

4

"The tadpoles have grown, too!
Now they look like little frogs.
Do you remember when they were tadpoles?
This is what they looked like."

How many little frogs can you
find in the pond? Count them.

6

Beachcombing

The waves carry shells and other things from the ocean onto the beach. Can you find these things in the sand?

Guy Smiley's Wonderful Weather Show

This is Guy Smiley, the world's favorite game show host, welcoming you to the WONDERFUL WEATHER SHOW! Yeah!

The first question is:
What's all around you but can't be seen, tasted, or smelled?
Air! That's right. The air you breathe. Here's a jar of it.

The second question is:
What is a cloud?
And the answer is: billions of tiny drops of water and tiny specks of dust that float in the air.

And now,
What is wind?
Right! You're right! Wind is moving air. The only time you can feel air is when it's windy! A storm called a hurricane brings very strong winds.

What is a tornado?
A funnel-shaped cloud with very strong, swirling winds.

The next question is:
What is rain?
Drops of water which fall from the clouds.

What is a flash of light in the sky during a rainstorm?
It's lightning, caused by electricity in the air.

What is the noise you usually hear after a flash of lightning?
How did you know? YES! It's THUNDER!

And now, FOR THE GRAND PRIZE, the last question is:

What is snow?
Water in clouds that freezes and falls to the earth as snowflakes. You did it! You won! So here's your prize from GUY SMILEY'S WONDERFUL WEATHER SHOW...a year's supply, that is 365 days, of... FREE WEATHER!

Did you know that no two snowflakes are exactly alike?

Right. Hold out your mitten and look closely. See? Each snowflake is different.

Grover's Pond

"All my little friends at the pond are going away for the winter. The ducks are flying to a warm place. The frogs are busy making holes deep in the mud at the bottom of the pond. They will sleep there until it is spring."

"Oh, look what I found! A feather! I will keep it to remind me that the ducks will be back when the weather is warm again."

Grover found a feather at the pond. Can you find these other things?

BIG BIRD'S BIRD FEEDER

"We could be out splashing people, and *you* want to stay here and hang peanut butter and seeds on your tree, Big Bird? If you ask me, it's for the birds!"

"Gosh, Oscar, how did you guess?"

Here's what you need to make an outdoor tree for your feathered friends:

6 wooden clip clothespins
6 heavy foil cupcake cups
½ cup of birdseed
¼ cup of peanut butter
½ cup of bacon fat or lard
1 cup of cornmeal
glue that won't dissolve in water
a grownup to help you

Here's what you do:

1. Melt the fat in a saucepan, and let it cool for a little while.
2. Add the birdseed, peanut butter, and cornmeal. Stir everything up with a wooden spoon.
3. Spoon some of the mixture into each foil cup.
4. Put the cups of bird cake in the refrigerator until they harden a bit.
5. Remove the cups from the refrigerator and put a blob of glue on the bottom of each cup. Glue each cup onto one flat side of a clothespin. Let the glue dry.
6. Pin the cakes onto the branches of a tree, and watch the birds enjoy their Christmas dinner!

Snow

It snowed all day;
It snowed all night.
Everything outside
Is covered in white!

Who walked through the snow
and where did they go?
Follow the footprints to find out.

Winter Fun

Some things in this picture are things to do in winter and some are not. Can you find three things in this picture that would be silly to do outside in winter?

The Four Seasons